The Boxcar Children® Mysteries

THE MYSTERY ON THE ICE

created by
GERTRUDE CHANDLER WARNER

Illustrated by Charles Tang

ALBERT WHITMAN & Company
Morton Grove, Illinois

Library of Congress Cataloging-in-Publication Data

Warner, Gertrude Chandler, 1890-1979
The mystery on the ice / created by
Gertrude Chandler Warner;
illustrated by Charles Tang.
p. cm. - (The Boxcar children mysteries)
Summary: The Alden children investigate when Mrs. Murray's jewels are
stolen during a party for the Starlight Skating Troupe.
ISBN 0-8075-5414-6 (hardcover).
ISBN 0-8075-5413-8 (paperback).
[1. Mystery and detective stories. 2. Ice skating–Fiction.
3. Brothers and sisters–Fiction.]
I. Tang, Charles, ill. II. Title. III. Series: Warner, Gertrude
Chandler, 1890 – Boxcar children mysteries.
PZ7.W244Mxs 1994
[Fic]–dc20
93-6302
CIP
AC

Cover art by David Cunningham.

Contents

CHAPTER 1

Exciting News

"Hurry, Benny," Jessie called from downstairs.

"I'm hurrying," six-year-old Benny answered, impatiently slicking down his hair. He wanted to look his best tonight for Joe and Alice Alden, their cousins, who had invited all the Aldens for a surprise celebration. What were they celebrating? He was glad Joe and Alice had moved from Pine Grove to Greenfield. He liked them a lot.

Violet poked her head in. "Are you

ready?" She paused. "You look handsome, Benny."

Benny grinned at her as he followed her down the steps. "You look handsome, too, Violet."

Jessie, waiting at the bottom of the stairs, said, "Yes, Violet does look *pretty*."

Ten-year-old Violet, in her lavender sweater and jeans, beamed. Jessie, who was twelve, wore a white cotton shirt and a chocolate-brown sweater, which matched her long hair, and brown pants. Watch, their dog, sat by the door. He barked, hoping to go along.

"Not tonight, Watch," Violet said, patting his head.

Struggling into her ski jacket, Jessie said, "Grandfather's warming up the station wagon."

"Where's Henry?" Benny asked, looking around.

"In the car with Grandfather," Jessie replied, pulling the hood of her jacket over her head.

Benny put on his down jacket and pulled on his mittens. "I want to see what Joe and Alice are celebrating, don't you?"

"Yes!" Violet said. "It sounds like a surprise and I like surprises."

Jessie laughed, opening the door. "So do I." It was odd that Grandfather didn't act as if he was going to be surprised. Every time they mentioned the dinner at Joe and Alice's, he just gave a knowing little smile. She was certain he knew what was going on.

Benny ran down the walk, which was heaped with snow on either side. He'd helped Henry shovel this morning. He jumped into the backseat. "We're all together and we're off to a celebration!" he shouted, sitting next to Jessie.

Grandfather glanced back at his grandson. "That's right, Benny." He smiled, pleased that his grandchildren always got along with one another so well.

The car wheels crunched over the packed snow on the short drive through town. Benny watched wide-eyed as they passed sparkling windows filled with toys. In the town square a huge Christmas tree towered, gleaming with red and green lights. Next to the tree stood a giant menorah, its candles casting light over the glistening snow.

When they reached the edge of Greenfield where Joe and Alice lived, fluffy snowflakes had started to drift onto the ground.

"Good weather for ice skating," Jessie said.

"Better weather for hockey," Henry teased, his eyes sparkling. He knew, though, that Jessie was the best and most graceful skater of them all.

"Here we are, children," Grandfather said, parking before an old, gray-shingled, three-story house. Tiny white lights twinkled on a pine tree on the spacious lawn.

"Doesn't the house look beautiful?" Violet said. "It's very different from the way it was when Joe and Alice first bought it." She giggled. "Remember Joe's foot breaking through the porch step?"

Henry got out, opening the back car door for Benny and the girls. "We did a lot of work on the old Roth house before Joe and Alice moved in," he said.

"We sure did! And remember we thought the house was haunted," Benny said, running alongside Henry on the way to the front door. Lifting the eagle door knocker, which was framed by a large evergreen wreath, Benny waited. He stomped first one booted foot, then another.

"You children have cleaned many places," Grandfather said. "The deserted library and . . ."

"The old motel," Violet added. "But each place was different. It's fun to see the before and after."

"Don't forget we stayed by ourselves in the boxcar," Henry said. "Remember, we ran away, so we wouldn't have to live with a grandfather we'd never known." He paused, smiling. "We didn't realize how lucky we were when Grandfather found us."

"That's right!" Benny said emphatically.

Just then Alice flung wide the front door. "I thought I heard voices."

"Come in," Joe said. "Let me take your coats."

"How wonderful everything is," Jessie exclaimed, admiring the many candles and the lovely red carpet. Two crimson wingback chairs nestled before the fireplace.

Violet walked over to the fire to warm her hands. She gazed above the mantel at the portrait of a young girl. This was the girl who had once lived here and had run away to marry against her father's wishes. "I see you've hung Celia Roth's painting."

"Yes," Joe said, standing beside her. "She's part of the house. We've become good friends with Celia, you know. And even though she's old and doesn't get around very well, she visits us every so often."

Alice joined them, and Joe slipped his arm around her waist. "I'm glad we bought this house. At first I was afraid it might need too much work."

"You've changed it into a charming home," Grandfather said.

Benny sniffed. "I smell something good," he hinted.

Alice leaned down. "You're not hungry, are you, Benny?"

He peered up at her. "A little," he admitted.

Joe laughed. "Maybe roast beef and mashed potatoes will satisfy your appetite."

Benny looked up, nodding vigorously.

Soon everyone was seated around the dining-room table. Benny piled his plate with broccoli, beef, and potatoes, then helped himself to a hot biscuit.

"This salad is delicious," Violet said shyly.

"Thanks, Violet," Alice said, setting cranberry sauce by Benny's elbow.

Once cake and ice cream were served, Joe cleared his throat. "I've invited everyone here to share our good news." He gazed with affection at Alice.

"What is it?" Benny leaned forward, his eyes big.

"Something wonderful," Joe said. "Your grandfather and his lawyer have worked with

Alice and me to bring us a child from Korea."

"Yes, we are flying to Seoul in two days to pick up a little Korean girl we are going to adopt," Alice said, her pretty face glowing.

"Her name is Soo Lee and she is seven years old," Joe said, a broad smile lighting his face, too.

"A little girl!" exclaimed Jessie.

Questions flew back and forth. All evening they discussed Joe and Alice's adopted daughter. How would she like American food? How would she be dressed? Would she understand English? Would she make friends at school?

When it was time to leave, Joe and Alice kissed their cousins. Joe shook Grandfather's hand. "Thanks for all your help, Uncle James. I see you can keep a secret. I've never seen such surprised faces!"

Standing in the doorway, Alice waved. "We'll see you on our return."

Once in the car, Benny asked, "What does adopted mean?"

"Adopted means to take someone into your home," Henry explained. "Someone to be your very own, because the child's parents can't take care of her or him."

"And," Grandfather continued, "papers will be signed showing that Joe and Alice are the child's legal parents."

Benny's round face wore a puzzled frown. "What does legal mean?" he questioned, cocking his head.

"Legal means that 'by law' Joe and Alice will be recognized as Soo Lee's mother and father," Jessie said.

"Oh," Benny said, sinking back against the seat. "I guess I understand."

That night, Jessie pulled up her comforter and stared out the window. She tried to imagine what the Korean child would be like. She was sure Soo Lee would be happy to be welcomed into such a warm and loving home. She wondered where Korea was exactly. She knew the country was near China, but she wanted to know more about it. Tomorrow they must go to the library and find all the information they could on Korea.

But the next morning, Grandfather had even more news — news so exciting that Jessie changed her mind about going to the library.

CHAPTER 2

The Murrays' Party

When the children came down for breakfast, Grandfather glanced up from his newspaper. "Mrs. McGregor set four places for you and left the oatmeal on the stove," he said, finishing his coffee. "She went to spend the holidays with her sister in Oregon."

Violet sipped her orange juice. "We don't need a housekeeper," she said. "We'll cook for you, Grandfather."

James Alden chuckled. "I'm afraid you'll be on your own most of the time. For the next week, I'll be attending meetings of the hospital directors." Then he added with a twinkle in his eye, "Do you think you can manage?"

"Oh, I think so," Henry said, rising and filling each bowl with oatmeal and raisins.

"Yes, we've been on our own thousands of times," Benny said.

Henry laughed. "Not quite that many, but we can cook, clean house, shop, and run errands," he said with pride in his voice.

"Good!" Grandfather said, pushing back his chair and standing. "Then I'm off to a committee meeting. I knew I needn't worry about you." He paused, a smile spreading across his face. "I almost forgot." He pulled an envelope from his pocket. "You know," he continued, "that I'm on the board of directors of Greenfield Hospital. Well, a skating troupe is coming to town to do a holiday benefit performance for the hospital."

"A *skating troupe* coming here!" Jessie exclaimed. If there was anything she loved it was ice skating! She enjoyed gliding across the ice, and she loved watching excellent skaters.

"Oh, boy!" Benny clapped his hands. "May we go and see the ice skaters?"

Grandfather laughed. "Better than that, Benny." He handed the envelope to Violet.

Violet opened the flap and pulled out a heavy card with gold printing.

"Read it," Henry urged.

Clearing her throat, Violet read: "To James Alden and Guests. You are invited to a party for the Starlight Skating Troupe. Thursday, December 27. 7:30. William and Sara Murray. 222 White Oak Lane."

Jessie sank back in her chair. The Starlight Troupe! One of the best skating shows in the country!

Between mouthfuls of toast, Benny said, "I like ice skaters, too." His eyes shone.

Grandfather nodded, happy to see their reaction. "I know you'll enjoy them. Not only that, but the skaters will be practicing all week at the Civic Center. You can watch them whenever you want."

Jessie gasped with pleasure. "I can't believe it," she said.

"Are the skaters in town now?" Henry inquired.

"They arrive this afternoon," James Alden answered. "We'll meet them tonight at the Murrays. You remember my good friends, William and Sara. They'll be delighted to see you again."

"You mean we're invited, too?" Violet asked in a soft voice.

Grandfather smiled. "I wouldn't go without you. You *all* are the 'guests' in the invitation."

"I suppose I have to get dressed up." Benny wrinkled his nose. "Don't I?"

James Alden nodded. "It's a special party. You want to look your best when you meet the ice skaters, don't you, Benny?"

"Sure." His round face brightened. "Maybe they'll teach me how to skate backward."

"I think," Henry said, "that first you should learn to skate forward."

"I know how to skate forward!" Benny protested in a loud voice.

"Yes, you do, Benny," Violet said, smiling. "But don't you think you could be a little more steady on your feet?"

Benny glanced at Violet, reluctantly agreeing. "I guess so. I want to skate without falling down so many times."

That afternoon the children went to the grocery store, then Henry read a mystery, Benny and Violet worked on a jigsaw puzzle, and Jessie wrote a letter to Aunt Jane.

In the late afternoon they made a light supper of toasted ham-and-cheese sandwiches and milk. They knew more food would be served at the party.

At seven o'clock, Jessie was the first one ready, so she sat by the fireplace, waiting for the others. She read and petted Watch, who snuggled next to her on the loveseat. She was looking especially pretty tonight, wearing a hair clip that had been a gift from Grandfather. She wore a blouse and skirt.

Soon Violet, in a green velvet dress, joined

Jessie. "What! No lavender?" Jessie teased.

"Not tonight," Violet said, sitting on a footstool before the fire. "This is my holiday dress."

Henry appeared the most grown-up in his gray blazer and navy trousers.

Benny rushed in. "I'm ready." His hair was neatly combed, and he was wearing a navy jacket and gray pants.

Grandfather was elegant in his tuxedo and bow tie. He held out two elbows to escort Jessie and Violet to the car.

When they arrived at the arched doorway of the Murrays' mansion, a woman in black, with a white apron and cap, opened the door and took their coats. Violet gasped at the large oak-paneled hall, the glittering crystal chandeliers, and the flames dancing in the marble fireplace.

Benny admired the toy soldiers lined up on the mantelpiece.

A tall woman, with white hair piled on top of her head, held out her arms and came toward them. "James! How nice to see you!"

She brushed Grandfather's cheek with a quick kiss. Then she smiled at the younger Aldens. "I haven't seen your grandchildren for some time. Let's see," she said, tapping a ringed finger on her chin, "this is Jessie, and Violet, and, oh, my," she paused to gaze at Henry, "how tall you've grown, Henry, and this is . . . is . . . ."

"Benny!" Benny piped up.

"Of course. Benny," Sara said.

Wide-eyed, Benny stared at Sara. "You shine more than all the holiday lights put together," he marveled.

"I guess I do," Mrs. Murray said with a laugh, touching her diamond necklace. Her dangling diamond earrings, diamond ring, and ruby bracelet shimmered in the light.

William Murray hurried to greet them. "The Aldens! I've been waiting for you! I want you to meet our honored guests, the ice skaters." William Murray and James Alden were the same age, but there the resemblance ended. James was tall, William was short and chubby.

William patted Benny on the back. "Make yourself at home, young man."

"I will," Benny promised.

After welcoming the other children, William left with James for a discussion in the study.

Jessie craned her neck, attempting to spot the ice skaters. In the center of the room, a small blonde woman chatted with an attractive young man. Apparently they were members of the troupe.

But before Jessie introduced herself, a plump woman with short black hair bustled up to Sara Murray. "Have you seen Ollie Olson?" she asked. "I can't keep track of him."

"The last I saw of Ollie, the clown," Mrs. Murray said, "he was filling his plate at the buffet table."

"Aha!" the frowning woman exclaimed. "I knew it! He's breaking training again!"

Mrs. Murray introduced each Alden. "Children, meet Janet O'Shea, the owner of the Starlight Troupe."

Janet, however, scarcely noticed the children. "I must find Ollie," she said, pressing her lips firmly together. "I'm sending him back to the hotel!" She strode off, leaving the Aldens to stare after her.

A short time later she passed by with a skinny man, who towered over her. They walked swiftly through the room. Janet was saying, "Go back to the hotel! And don't order room service! I can't afford it!" That must be Ollie with Miss O'Shea, Jessie thought.

The clown skater gave Janet a mock bow and was gone before they could meet him.

"Ollie's impossible!" Janet muttered.

What a rude woman, Jessie thought. If the other skaters were like her, she didn't care whether she met them or not!

CHAPTER 3

Unwelcome News

When Sara Murray asked the Aldens if they'd like to meet a pair of skaters, Jessie forgot about the unfriendly owner of the troupe.

Mrs. Murray steered Jessie, her brothers, and sister through the crowd and over to the same blonde woman and young man Jessie had seen earlier. "This is Alexandra Patterson and Carl Underhill. Carl used to play hockey."

Alexandra turned, pleased to meet the Aldens. Carl, just as friendly as Alexandra, shook hands with each of them.

From the way Carl gazed at Alexandra and the way Alexandra's eyes lit up when she looked at Carl, Violet thought the two were in love.

"You're lucky to live in Greenfield," Alexandra said, holding a pink rose, a shade darker than her chiffon dress. "From what I've seen, it's a lovely town."

Jessie kept staring at Alexandra. Finally she said, "We like it here. Where are you from, Alexandra?"

"I'm from Chicago, the Windy City. And, please call me Alex." The dainty girl's laugh tinkled lightly on the air. All at once she dropped her rose. Carl stooped to retrieve it, but Henry had already scooped it up and returned it to her.

"Why, thank you, Henry," Alex said, her green eyes sparkling with pleasure.

Amazed, Benny watched as a flush of crimson crept over Henry's face.

"Ever play hockey?" Carl asked.

"Wh-what?" Henry stammered, still gazing at Alex.

"Ever play hockey?" Carl repeated.

At last Henry turned to Carl. "Yes. I like hockey."

"Good. Is there a place we can play outdoors?"

"Down at Burton's Park," Benny said. "The city floods it in the winter. All the kids skate there."

"Sounds good," Carl said. "How about a game?"

"You name the time," Henry said. "I know you need to practice."

"Oh, yes." Carl glanced at Janet O'Shea. "Boss lady is cracking the whip. The company could go under if our show doesn't earn more money." He paused, then grinned. "But we'll play on Tuesday. How about it?"

"A game with you would be great," Henry responded. "I'm sure you can teach me the finer points of hockey."

"Me, too." Benny rubbed his chin. "First, though, I'm too wobbly. I need to learn how to stand up long enough to hit the puck."

Carl laughed. "We'll work on that, Benny." He thought a second. "What time on Tuesday?"

"Two o'clock, okay?" Henry said.

"You've got it," Carl said.

"Hi!" A young girl on crutches hobbled up to them, her red curls bobbing. "I'm Marcia Westerly," she said, holding out her hand. "I overheard your names." She smiled. "I'm new to the company."

"Were you in a skating troupe before?" Violet asked.

"Yes, the Moonbeams. But I'm sure you've never heard of us. You see, I'm from Winnipeg, Canada."

Jessie knew almost all the famous skating groups, but she'd never heard of the Moonbeams.

"I haven't had a chance to skate with Carl and Alex," Marcia said, holding up a crutch. "I'd better start soon, though, or I'll be too rusty to skate."

Violet smiled. "I think it's like riding a

bicycle. Once you know how, you can pick it up no matter how long it's been."

Marcia winced as she shifted a foot.

"Did you fall on the ice?" Benny questioned, looking at her bandaged ankle.

"Yes, I tried a triple jump and landed in a heap." She shook her head, apparently reliving her awful fall. She looked sad, but when a maid offered a trayful of tiny tuna sandwiches, Marcia broke into a smile. "I'm starved," she said.

The maid announced, "The buffet table is ready."

"Let's go," Benny said, heading for the dining room.

Henry laughed. "One mention of food and Benny is off and running."

But when the others caught up with Benny they were overwhelmed by the lavish display of smoked salmon, baked ham, and roast turkey. Cranberry-and-nut bread, hot biscuits, and relishes were at one end of the long table, and pasta and vegetables at the other. A chef wearing a tall white hat stood behind the

table. "What would you like?" he asked.

Benny pointed to the turkey.

The chef carved a slice of turkey and placed it on Benny's plate.

"And could I have a little ham, please?" Benny asked.

"You may have as much as you like," the chef said, cutting a generous piece of ham.

Benny waited as the chef drizzled pineapple juice over his ham. Then in a bolder voice he asked, "And some salmon?"

The chef gave a hearty laugh. "I like to see a good appetite."

Henry, Violet, and Jessie followed Benny. Their heaping plates were just as full as Benny's.

They sat down at a small table and began to eat. "Did you see the desserts?" Jessie said.

Benny glanced up. "Where?"

"Right behind you," Violet said, smiling. "I hope you saved room!"

Benny whirled about. He loved desserts. His eyes grew big. A chocolate cake, decorated with strawberries, was surrounded by several pies and many kinds of holiday cookies. "Oh, boy!" Benny said. "I'm having a gingerbread boy and a reindeer and some cake!"

They all laughed.

The party had been lots of fun, and on the way home the children scarcely noticed that it had begun to snow heavily. All they could talk about was the wonderful food, the beautiful mansion, and the ice skaters.

That night, after Violet had gone to bed, she lay awake, thinking about the grand party.

In the morning the surprised children awoke to mounds of flying snow and a howling wind.

Mr. Alden greeted his grandchildren at breakfast. "Today I'll be working in my office. I have a number of calls to make."

"You're not going out?" Benny asked.

"Not today. Because of the blizzard, most roads are blocked and highways closed."

"A blizzard!" Henry said, looking out the window at the sea of white.

"Yes," Mr. Alden said. "I'm afraid it's bad

out." He hesitated. "I have more bad news."

Jessie looked at Grandfather expectantly.

"What's the bad news?" asked Benny.

"I just got a call from William. The Murrays were burglarized last night. After everyone left the party and the Murrays went to bed, someone broke in and stole Sara's jewelry. She discovered the theft this morning."

"Oh, no!" Violet dropped into a chair. "*Not* Mrs. Murray's beautiful jewels!"

Grandfather nodded. "All her diamonds and a ruby bracelet were stolen. She had left them in her dressing room. She said she had forgotten to lock the drawer she kept them in. Of course, the Murrays called the police."

Grandfather slipped on his sweater. "I'll be working late, but if you need me, don't be afraid to interrupt me." He turned and went back upstairs, saying, "Take care, children. Let's be sure our doors are locked."

Benny checked the front and back doors. "Now no one can get in here!"

After Grandfather left, the children sat silently at the breakfast table. At last Jessie said, "Who would rob the Murrays?"

"I don't know," Henry said. "It's hard to understand." He bit his lip, remembering Grandfather's warning about locking their own doors. Did a thief actually skulk about in quiet Greenfield?

"Let's see if we can hear the weather forecast," Violet said, jumping up to turn the dial on the kitchen radio. An announcer was saying, "All highways going in and out of Greenfield are impassable. The airport is closed until further notice. Do not travel today unless it's an emergency. The storm is expected to last another three to four hours."

"Will we be all right?" Benny asked in a worried voice.

Jessie smiled. "We'll be warm and cozy. The storm won't last forever." She glanced outside at the weather. At least the robber couldn't escape from Greenfield. But who could it be? She hoped it wasn't one of the ice skaters. Could it have been one of the guests?

CHAPTER 4

Blizzard

While the wind howled and the snow blew, Violet cleared the table. Henry washed the breakfast dishes, Jessie dried, and Benny placed plates in the cupboard.

"I wonder who stole Mrs. Murray's jewels?" Jessie asked, drying a pink cup and handing it to Benny.

"Someone very mean!" Benny said, carefully putting his precious cup on the shelf. Even though it was cracked and old, that pink cup had been with him ever since his boxcar days.

"Maybe one of the ice skaters stole Mrs. Murray's diamonds, or it could have been Miss O'Shea, or just a robber from Greenfield," Benny said.

"Hmmm," Henry speculated. "It could be the maid or even the Murrays themselves."

"The Murrays!" Benny looked startled. "Why would they steal their very own diamonds?"

"Insurance money," Henry said simply. "After all, we don't know if William Murray needs money or not." He noticed Benny's downcast face. "Although I doubt it. It's a pretty farfetched idea, but we need to think of *all* the angles. That's what a detective does."

"Maybe Carl is the thief," Violet said. But she hated the thought that such a friendly young man would steal from his hosts.

"We've got to suspect everyone. Even Alex might have stolen Mrs. Murray's gems," Jessie said in a doubtful voice.

A plate slipped out of Henry's hands back

into the soapsuds. "No, no, she's too delicate."

Jessie gave a teasing laugh. "You don't have to be a weight lifter to carry away a bag of diamonds and rubies."

"I'll bet Janet O'Shea is the guilty one!" Benny said. "She never smiles!"

"Shhh!" Violet said, placing a finger to her lips. "Listen!"

The Aldens stood still, trying to catch every word of the radio announcer:

"Last night while the storm raged and the citizens of Greenfield slept, a burglary happened on White Oak Lane. The thief broke through a downstairs window, climbed in, and escaped with over $150,000 worth of jewels from an upstairs dressing room. As of now, the police have no suspects."

Henry said, "We need to think about anyone who noticed Mrs. Murray's diamonds."

"Who *wouldn't* notice her diamonds?" Benny said. "She looked like a bright neon sign!"

Violet smiled. Benny always went right to the point.

"One hundred fifty thousand dollars!" Benny whistled. "That's a lot of money!"

"It certainly is!" Jessie agreed. "I hope we can help find Mrs. Murray's jewels. She's such a nice person."

When the dishes were finished, the children went into the living room. They watched the snow whirl about the house and listened to the wind tear at the trees.

"What should we do today?" Benny asked, sinking into the rocker. "I don't want to fit together any more jigsaw puzzles."

"I know," Violet said. "Let's look up Korea in the encyclopedia."

"That's a good idea," Jessie said. "I wanted to go to the library, but today's not the day!" She left the room to gather a few books from the den.

"I wonder where Joe and Alice are now," Henry said. "Just think — they're halfway around the world."

"Have they *adopted* Soo Lee yet?" Benny

asked, proud of himself for using the new word he'd learned.

"Not yet," Violet said. "I imagine they'll be busy locating Soo Lee, signing papers, and packing Soo Lee's belongings."

Benny nodded. "I wonder if she wears clothes like ours."

"Let's find out," Jessie said, re-entering the room. Under her arm she carried a fat encyclopedia and an atlas.

They spent the morning reading about Korea's crops, food, houses, and government. Next they pored over a map of Asia.

"Korea is northeast of China." With her finger, Jessie traced the outline of Korea. "See, the Korean Peninsula is surrounded by water on three sides: the Yellow Sea, the Sea of Japan, and the East China Sea."

"Korea isn't very far from Japan," Henry said. "It's only separated by a narrow strait of water."

"Joe and Alice flew here," Violet said, pointing to a city called Seoul. "Seoul is the capital of Korea."

"What's that line in the center of the country?" Benny asked.

"Korea is divided into North Korea and South Korea, Joe and Alice are in South Korea," Violet explained.

"Wow!" Benny said. "They're so far away!"

"They'll be home before you know it, Benny!" Henry said with a chuckle. "That's the advantage of flying."

"Soo Lee must be a puzzled little girl," Violet said thoughtfully.

"Or an excited one!" Jessie added.

"I'd be excited about coming to America," Benny said.

"I would, too!" Henry said, placing a hand on Benny's shoulder. Benny grinned at his big brother.

"The wind has died down," Jessie said, cocking her head and listening.

Violet leaped up and looked out the window. "And it's not snowing so hard."

Henry went to get his sheepskin jacket and lined boots. "Let's shovel the walk," he said.

"Yea!" Benny cheered, dashing to the closet for his down jacket and pants.

Dressed in their warmest clothes, they all hurried outside with Watch prancing at their side.

"Look at me!" Benny shouted, wading into the deep snow. He lay on his back atop a drift and moved his arms and feet in a wide arc. "There!" he said, getting up carefully. "See my angel!"

"Very nice," Jessie said, lightly tossing a snowball at her little brother.

Soon the children were flinging snowballs at one another in a rousing fight. Watch dashed from one to the other, leaping in the air. His muzzle was white with snow.

Then the Aldens took turns shoveling a pathway on the walk.

"Let's go to the Civic Center and watch the ice skaters," Jessie said.

"How are we going to get there?" Benny asked, staring at the snow surrounding them. Branches and telephone wires, heavy with snow, sagged to the breaking point. No cars were traveling on the road past their house.

"We'll wade through the snow over to Main Street," Jessie said. "The snowplow will have cleared important streets so buses can run. We can catch a bus and get off at the Civic Center. And let's take our skates."

The children flung their skates over their shoulders and hurried to catch the bus.

When they arrived at the Civic Center, Violet was delighted to see Carl and Alex, hand in hand, gliding over the ice. The two graceful skaters moved in time to a waltz.

At one point Carl lifted Alex overhead. With her arms outstretched, Alex looked like a ballet dancer.

When the music stopped, Carl gently set Alex down. For a moment they smiled at each other. "Oh, Carl and Alex are so in love," Violet said softly.

Benny rolled his eyes. "That's mushy stuff, Violet," he said in a disgusted voice.

Carl and Alex skated over to the bench where the children were lacing up their skates.

"Your routine was beautiful," Jessie said. "I wish I knew how to spin like that."

Alex laughed, holding out her hand. "I'll teach you." She turned to Violet. "You come, too," she urged.

"You go ahead. I broke a shoelace," Violet said.

Jessie skimmed over the ice to warm up.

Alex clapped. "You have a fine skating form, Jessie. Would you like some lessons?"

"Oh, yes!" Jessie exclaimed. To be taught by a professional skater was a dream come true.

While Alex and Jessie practiced spins at one end of the rink, Carl, Henry, and Benny tried different hockey strokes at the other end.

In another part of the rink, Ollie, the clown, was skating backward. His trousers were too short, and his yellow-and-red shirt flopped about his long arms. He stumbled, waving his arms to stay upright. He swayed back and forth and staggered forward, slipping and sliding to keep his balance. Benny laughed. He laughed even harder when the clown tumbled to the ice, then bounced back up. Everyone laughed and clapped. Ollie lifted his round hat in appreciation, then skittered and tottered all the way to the dressing room.

Violet tied a knot in her broken lace, then skated back and forth in front of the stands. When she stopped to rest, holding onto the railing, she saw Janet O'Shea talking to a man in the top row of seats. The man wore a black topcoat and a big-brimmed black hat pulled down so far that it hid his face. He kept looking around nervously as if he didn't want to be seen.

How strange, Violet thought. She'd never seen the man before, and Janet O'Shea's worried frown puzzled her. Could the mystery man have anything to do with the Murrays' robbery?

CHAPTER 5

The Mystery Man

After skating at the Civic Center, the Aldens joined Carl and Alex for hot chocolate in the coffee shop next door. Marcia, who sat alone drinking coffee, limped over on her crutches.

"May I sit with you?" she asked.

"Sure, Marcia." Jessie moved over. "There's plenty of room."

Violet sipped her chocolate. "I saw a man in black talking to Janet O'Shea," she said in a soft voice. "I couldn't see his face, but Janet looked worried."

"That man wearing a black cowboy hat?" Carl said. "I've seen him around, too. I can't figure out why he's always watching us."

"Maybe he stole the diamonds!" Benny piped up.

Carl gave a nervous laugh. "I don't know about that, Benny."

Henry glanced at Carl. Why did he seem nervous at the mention of diamonds? He hoped Carl wasn't the thief. He liked him. And, being a former hockey player, Carl was a terrific ice skater. He could dodge and race around the rink better than anyone Henry had ever seen.

Marcia agreed with Benny. "I think that mystery man may be the guilty one, too. He *acts* like a thief."

Alex pushed her cup aside. "Just because someone looks different doesn't mean he's a criminal. Anyway, the police will find the guilty man."

"Or woman," Jessie suggested.

"Or woman," Alex agreed. Then changing the subject, she said, "I need to stitch rhinestones on my costume before our Friday night performance."

"What color is your outfit?" Violet asked.

"As red as Marcia's hair," Alex said with a light laugh.

Marcia ran her fingers through her red bangs. "I hate this color. I always wanted to be blonde like you, Alex."

"One thing for sure, your red hair would clash with my crimson costume," Alex added.

"Yes," Marcia admitted. "My green one is the right color for me." She sighed. "Too bad I won't have a chance to wear it."

"That's a shame, Marcia. Your costume is beautiful," Alex said.

Violet said, "Oh, I'd love to see it!"

"I knew you would," Jessie said, smiling. "Violet is an artist and loves to paint."

"Violet helped me pick out my T-shirt," Benny said, beaming. "I like blue."

Alex's eyes sparkled. "We could use some help backstage, Violet. Would you like to see the costumes and maybe do a little repair work?"

"I'd love to!" Violet beamed at the prospect.

"Fine," Alex said, standing. "Why doesn't everyone come back to the Civic Center tomorrow morning. Jessie and I will continue our lessons, the boys can play hockey, and Violet will check out the costumes."

"Don't forget we're playing hockey in the afternoon, too!" Benny reminded Carl.

"Burton's Park, right?" Carl said. "Two o'clock. I won't forget."

"You're invited, too," Henry said, turning to Jessie and Violet. He smiled shyly at Alex. "You, too, Alex."

"We'll be there," Jessie said.

"Wonderful," Carl said. "We'll have a good game."

Jessie turned to Marcia, not wanting her to feel left out of the conversation. "I see Valentina Markov is starring in the New York Ice Show. She's an older skater, but still one of the best, don't you think?"

Marcia stared at Jessie. "Who?"

"Valentina Markov," Jessie repeated.

"I don't remember her," Marcia said, reaching for her crutches and preparing to leave. "But I have to admit, I'm not very good about remembering names."

Jessie raised her eyebrows. An ice skater who hadn't heard of Valentina Markov wasn't much of an ice skater!

" 'Bye, everyone," Marcia said, leaving as quickly as she could on her crutches.

As Carl and Alex turned to go back to the hotel, Henry noticed a brochure sticking out of Carl's hip pocket. The title caught Henry's eye: *DIAMONDS!* He poked Jessie and pointed at Carl's retreating back.

Jessie's eyes widened. "Why is he reading about diamonds?"

"Who's reading about diamonds?" Benny asked, looking from Henry to Jessie.

"Carl," Jessie answered.

"Carl is reading about diamonds?" Violet echoed in disbelief.

"I'm afraid so," Henry said. "I saw a brochure in his back pocket."

Benny bit his lip. "That looks bad, doesn't it?"

"But it doesn't prove anything. Carl probably has a reason," Henry said, not wanting to upset Benny. But it was hard to keep the doubt out of his voice. Not only had Carl acted nervous when the word "diamonds" was mentioned, but he was also studying them!

"I'll bet Janet O'Shea stole the diamonds and rubies," Benny said, wanting everyone to forget about Carl.

"She does need money to save the Starlight Troupe," Violet said, "but I can't imagine she's a thief."

"What about Marcia?" said Jessie. "She is certainly a strange ice skater. I've never heard of her troupe, the Moonbeams, and when I mentioned Valentina Markov, she'd never heard of her."

"I think we can rule out Marcia as a suspect," said Henry. "Can you see her climbing through a window and going upstairs on crutches?"

Jessie smiled. "I guess the idea is pretty wild."

Violet reached for her jacket. "We'd better catch the bus, and start supper."

When the Aldens opened their front door, they were pleased to see Grandfather in front of the fire, reading.

After a brief chat, the children started supper. Jessie put a chicken in the oven, Henry peeled potatoes, Violet shredded cabbage for coleslaw, and Benny shelled peas.

At the dinner table, Henry asked Grandfather how William and Sara Murray were getting along.

"They're a little better," James Alden said, "although Sara is naturally sad to lose her jewels. Many years ago her grandmother gave her the ruby bracelet."

Henry hesitated. "I hate to ask, Grandfather, but could Mr. Murray have hidden the jewels and just *pretended* they'd been stolen? Maybe he needs the insurance money."

Grandfather threw back his head and laughed. "No, no, Henry. William has just donated a very large sum to build a new wing on the hospital. He's a wealthy man." Then Mr. Alden sobered. "I know that you are just trying to find the thief. Everyone must be considered a suspect."

Henry was glad Grandfather understood. It was awkward to accuse Grandfather's friend.

"What do we have for dessert?" Benny asked, looking up and down the table, after he'd eaten his dinner.

"Are you able to eat dessert after two pieces of chicken, coleslaw, mashed potatoes and gravy, and peas?" Amused, Violet waited for his answer, even though she knew what it would be.

"You bet!" Benny answered.

"We have chocolate ice cream with fudge topping," Jessie said.

Benny had an expectant look on his round face. "Anything else?"

"And peanut butter cookies," Jessie finished.

"Good!" Benny said, holding up his spoon.

The next day at the Civic Center, Jessie practiced twirling on skates, the boys played hockey, and Violet happily examined the beautiful skating costumes. Green, blue, gold, black, and silver ones hung on the rack. Her favorite was a lavender costume, dotted with purple stones. A few were decorated with feathers, but all glittered and sparkled with beads, sequins, and rhinestones.

Later, when the children were ready to leave, and all the skaters except Ollie had left the rink, Violet bent down and picked up a program. Startled, she noticed a crudely drawn map of Greenfield on the back. "Look at this," she whispered, handing the program to Jessie.

"I wonder who drew it," Jessie said. "Whoever it was underlined the Murray

house in green ink! *And* wrote, 'windows at ground level' on it."

Benny sank down on a bleacher seat, puzzling over this latest development.

Henry studied the map. "Who would have a copy of Friday night's skating program on Tuesday?"

"It could be Janet O'Shea! She's in charge of things," Benny said firmly, coming back to his prime suspect.

For a moment all that was heard were skates scraping on ice as Ollie practiced his spills.

"I'll keep this," said Henry. "Maybe it means something."

Jessie hoped the burglar was the mystery man, but now she wasn't sure. All the skaters were friends. She didn't want any of them to be guilty. But a shiver ran up her spine with the dreaded thought that *someone* in the troupe had stolen the jewels.

CHAPTER 6

Carl Under Suspicion

By Wednesday more snow had fallen, and although Greenfield was shoveling out, major highways and the airport still were closed.

The Aldens again rode the bus to the Civic Center. Along Main Street, the bus stopped at a red light. Jessie, gazing out the window, drew in a sharp breath. "There's Carl!" She pointed to a jewelry store, where Carl stood peering in the window.

"He's going into the shop!" Henry exclaimed.

"Why is he going into a jewelry store?" Benny questioned.

No one answered. "Oh," Benny said in a low voice. "I know. He's seeing how much diamonds and rubies are worth!" He felt sad.

Suddenly Benny jumped up and down in his seat. "Look! The mystery man!" he shouted.

Sure enough, leaning against a lamppost, the man with the black hat watched Carl disappear inside the shop. Now Violet could see he had a mustache.

"Why is he watching Carl?" Benny asked.

"I don't know," Jessie said. "Could he think Carl is the thief?"

At the Civic Center, Alex met them. "We have the rink to ourselves," Alex said. "There's no practice today."

"You mean we can play hockey on the whole rink?" Benny asked in an eager voice.

"The whole rink!" Alex repeated. "When Carl gets here, we'll begin." She looked around. "He's late. I wonder what's keeping him."

None of the Aldens said a word.

Oh, Jessie thought, if poor Alex only knew what Carl was up to!

Finally, Carl arrived. "Let's have a game!" he said, acting as if nothing was wrong! Violet frowned.

Jessie started to warm up, skimming to the opposite side, then back again.

Then they all began to play hockey. Henry, Alex, and Violet were on one team, and Carl, Jessie, and Benny on the other. The game started. Alex made a quick pass to Henry, and Henry hit the puck through Carl's legs.

"Good move!" yelled Carl.

Soon the puck was flying back and forth.

"Time out!" Benny yelled, sliding across the ice on his stomach. "I fell!"

He tried to get up, but his feet went out from under him and down he went again. "I'll get up this time!" he declared. But once more his skates slid back and forth, and he tumbled.

"Are you all right?" Henry asked, with concern, skating to Benny's side.

"I'm okay," Benny said, taking Henry's offered hand. Unsteadily, he stood, rubbing his hip. "It's my rear that's sore!"

Alex's gentle laugh rippled over the group. "That's the danger of being an ice skater!"

"But you don't fall as much as I do!" Benny complained.

"We did when we first learned to skate," Carl said with a chuckle.

For an hour they played hockey, then Marcia called, "Time for hot chocolate!"

"Everyone for hot chocolate say, 'Yes'!" Benny shouted.

"Yes!" everybody yelled, heading for the bench to remove their skates.

Walking over to the coffee shop, Jessie lagged behind with Marcia. "It's too bad you can't play hockey. It's such fun." She hesitated. "Tell me, do you do the camel spin in your routine?"

Marcia shook her head.

"How about the double or triple axel?"

"Both," she said.

"And the salchow?" Jessie asked.

"What's a salchow?" Marcia asked. "I'm from Canada. I'm not familiar with that term."

Jessie had thought all ice skaters knew what a salchow was. But maybe the term wasn't used in Canada.

"A salchow is a one-revolution jump," she explained.

"I see," said Marcia. She was staring at the courtyard, next to the Civic Center, where several snow sculptures had been made. "Isn't that clever?" she asked, pointing to an unfinished mermaid.

Jessie just nodded.

As they were about to leave the coffee shop, Henry held up his hand. "Wait. Carl is in the courtyard, working on an ice sculpture."

Sure enough, Carl was shaping the mermaid's face, stopping every so often to nervously glance about.

"Why does he keep looking over his shoulder?" Benny asked.

"He doesn't want anyone to see him." Henry narrowed his eyes. "Look! He's hiding something in the mermaid's hand."

Jessie said, "Let's find out Carl's secret." She paused, watching Carl pat snow over the sculpture's hand. "We'll wait until he leaves."

Carl stepped back and examined his work. Then, with a final look around, he walked into the rink office.

The Aldens hurried outside. Benny dashed ahead to the ice mermaid. He dug into her snowy hand and held up a bright object.

"Wh-why," Violet stammered in disbelief, "it's a diamond ring!"

In astonishment the Aldens stared at the ring, sparkling in the sun.

"Put it in your pocket, Violet," Henry urged, "before Carl returns. This is one diamond he won't be able to sell!" He felt disappointed. His friend had betrayed him!

CHAPTER 7

The Diamond Ring

Sadly, Violet slipped the diamond ring in her pocket. It was hard to believe Carl was a thief. "We'd better go home and tell Grandfather," she said.

"I suppose you're right, Violet." Jessie felt sad, too.

"Wait!" Benny shouted. "I forgot my scarf!"

"Hurry back to the shop and get it," Henry said. "We need to catch the bus."

Benny ran inside and dashed back, his red scarf around his neck. "Hide! Hide!" he said, waving his arms in the air. "Carl is coming back!"

The Aldens rushed to hide behind some bushes.

Carl glanced around, then returned to his mermaid. He brushed the snow off the sculpture's hand. When he couldn't find the ring, he dug deeper. "Oh, no!" he said out loud. He bent down, scooping snow away from the base of the sculpture. "It has to be here! It has to!" His voice shook as he searched the ground.

Spying Benny's red scarf fluttering in the wind, Carl strode over. "What are you doing here?" he asked in a puzzled tone.

"Are you looking for something?" Benny asked.

"Yes, yes, I am," Carl admitted.

"Is this what you're searching for?" Violet asked, holding up the ring.

Carl's face lit up. "My diamond ring!" he exclaimed.

"Is it *your* diamond?" Henry asked. "Does it belong to *you*?"

Carl stared at Henry. "Of course, it's my diamond! I bought it at Morton's Jewelry Store!"

"You *bought* this ring?" Jessie asked.

"Yes," Carl answered. "The diamond is an engagement ring for Alex. I was planning to show her my ice sculpture and let her find the hidden ring!"

Sheepishly, the children looked at one another. Violet handed the ring to Carl.

Carl snapped his fingers in sudden understanding. "You thought *I* was the jewel thief?"

"We didn't *want* to think that!" Benny exclaimed quickly.

Carl heaved a happy sigh of relief. "I'm just glad to have the ring back." He chuckled. "I suppose I did look suspicious."

"Yes," Henry said. "You not only carried a lot of cash and went into a jewelry store, but you were nervous every time diamonds were mentioned." He grinned. "Now I know why."

Carl returned the ring to the mermaid,

nestling it in her hand and piling snow over it. "I'm still going ahead with my surprise. I asked Alex to meet me here."

"She'll be thrilled," Jessie said. "I'd love to see her face."

"Not me!" Benny said, shaking his head. "There will be kissing and hugging and all that gooey stuff!"

"That's true, Benny," Violet said with a shy smile. "We don't want to be in the way. This is between Carl and Alex."

Jessie nodded. "We were just leaving."

"Good luck, Carl," Henry said.

On the bus the children talked about mistaking Carl for a burglar.

"Now we can scratch Carl off our suspect list," Jessie said.

"Maybe we should concentrate on Janet O'Shea and the Mystery Man," Violet said.

"Yes!" Benny said in a loud voice. "Especially Janet O'Shea — because she's always frowning!"

"And we know she needs money to keep the troupe going," Jessie said.

* * *

The next morning, the Aldens arrived at the rink where Alex was skating. After finishing a figure eight, she skated over to the children. "I understand you knew about this before I did," she said, giving a silvery laugh and holding up her left hand. The diamond ring sparkled and glistened.

"Were you surprised?" Benny asked.

"Very surprised!" Alex replied. "I guess I'm the happiest person alive."

Jessie and Violet leaned over to study the beautiful ring.

Henry admired Alex's pretty, glowing face. "You and Carl make a good pair."

"And not only on the ice!" Jessie added, smiling. She was happy for Alex.

At the far end of the rink, Ollie was practicing his clown routine. He leaned forward in a lopsided spin.

"We forgot about Ollie!" Benny said. "Maybe *he* stole the diamonds!"

"Maybe," Alex said. "But he doesn't have much time. He practices a lot. He seems more interested in skating and making people laugh."

"I'm glad!" Benny said. "He's a funny clown!" But he wondered. How long did it take to crawl in a window and steal a bagful of jewels?

"There's Miss O'Shea," Henry said. "I wonder if she'd tell us who the man in black is."

"I hope you find what you're looking for," Alex said, skating backward. "You're good detectives!" She smiled. "I'm glad you know Carl is innocent!"

The Aldens left Alex and hurried over to Miss O'Shea.

"Hi, Miss O'Shea," Henry said.

Janet O'Shea turned. "What is it? I'm a busy woman!"

"We wondered about the man in black," Jessie said.

"The man in black?" She paused. "What do you want to know about him?"

Benny squinted up at her. "Maybe he's the robber."

"Oh!" The short plump woman sank down onto a seat.

"Is he with the troupe?" Violet asked. "We've seen him spying on people."

Janet O'Shea gazed at her fingertips. "I don't know who he is!"

Jessie thought this was strange! They had seen Janet talking to this man. Maybe Janet and the man had planned the robbery together!

Suddenly Jessie had a thought that hadn't occurred to her before. "Have there been other robberies besides the Murrays'?" she asked.

"Yes," Janet O'Shea answered. "In every town where we've performed, one of our wealthy patrons has been robbed."

"So," Jessie reasoned, "if anyone joined the troupe *after* the other robberies, that person would be in the clear."

Janet O'Shea's finger tapped her chin. "No one is *that* new to the troupe."

Janet O'Shea stood up. "Time to go to work. I've a pile of bills to go through." She shook her head. "I don't know how I'll pay my skaters."

She left, the Aldens staring after her.

"Hi, everyone!" Marcia hobbled toward them. "I've been working on my costume."

"Are you going to be off your crutches soon?" Benny wondered.

Marcia gazed at Benny. "Why?"

"I want to see you skate," he replied, folding his arms.

"I'd like to see you skate, too," Jessie said, taking a deep breath. There was no easy way to say what was on her mind. She couldn't come right out and say, "I think it's strange you don't remember Valentina Markov!"

Frowning, Marcia turned to face Jessie. "You think I stole Mrs. Murray's jewels, don't you?"

For a moment Jessie didn't reply, then she said slowly, "Did you?"

Marcia's frown changed to a smile. "You don't *really* believe I could crawl through a window, sneak upstairs, and steal jewels, do you?" She raised a crutch. "No way could I be the thief!"

"No," Henry agreed. "Being on crutches, you wouldn't be able to rob the Murrays."

"But we need to suspect everyone, Marcia," Violet added, not wanting to upset her.

"What about the mystery man?" Marcia questioned. "He spies on everyone. I don't trust him."

"We're wondering about him, too," Violet said.

Marcia shook her head and hobbled away.

"Let's go home," Benny said. "I want to build an ice sculpture like Carl's."

Violet laughed. "We might not be able to make something that pretty, but I'll bet we could build a great snowman!"

Benny grinned. "Good! But first I want to buy an apple in the coffee shop!"

They all went into the shop. As they were leaving, Jessie picked up a newspaper on the floor. Scanning the contents, she silently handed the paper to Henry.

"This is an article from the Greenfield paper," he said. "It's about the upcoming benefit performance." He read off the names of the listed board members. When he came to the Murrays' name, he stopped. "William Murray's name is circled in green ink," he said in an excited voice. "Just like the ink on that map of Greenfield we found."

"It looks as if *someone* was interested in the Murrays and their house," Violet said.

"Someone in the troupe?" Jessie asked.

Benny wrinkled his nose. "I don't like whoever did it!"

"Shall we build that snowman?" Henry said, patting Benny on the back. "We're getting closer and closer to finding the real thief." He tucked the article in his pocket.

Jessie hoped so. There were so many suspects, though, it was hard to figure out who could be the thief!

CHAPTER 8

A Dead End?

When they arrived home, the Aldens changed into old clothes, then hurried outdoors to build the biggest snowman on the block.

Watch romped at Benny's side, and Benny threw snow up in the air, letting it drift over him and the dog. Laughing, Benny plunged into a snowbank. Jessie pulled him out and dusted him off, saying with a chuckle, "We don't need to build a snowman. We'll just stand you in front of the house, Benny, and stick a broom in your hand."

"No, no!" Benny shouted, taking off his knit cap and shaking snowflakes out of his short brown hair. "We'll build a real snowman! Come on, Violet, let's roll a big snowball!"

Violet waded through the snow and joined him. Benny made a snowball, and together they rolled it over and over until the tiny ball grew and grew.

"Jessie," Henry said, "we can't let them get ahead of us. Let's roll a huge ball for the bottom of the snowman."

"Okay," Jessie said, hurrying to help him. They began to roll a second ball. Bigger and bigger it swelled.

Once Jessie and Henry's ball was in place, Violet and Benny set the smaller one on top. Now the snowman had a body, but no head.

"I'll roll the head!" Benny exclaimed, starting another snowball. Watch leaped and played alongside. His paws and muzzle were white with snow.

Henry formed snow-arms, then stuck the snow shovel through one.

When the snowman was complete, Violet added a carrot for the nose, purple grapes for eyes, and a slice of melon for the mouth.

Benny dashed inside and found an old hat, scarf, and gloves to decorate the snowman. Jessie finished it by adding five green apples for buttons.

"I could eat one of those apples right now," Benny said.

Henry laughed. "Shall we start supper?"

"Yes!" Benny said, snow covering him from head to foot, except for his rosy cheeks and twinkling eyes.

The children stamped snow from their boots before entering the house. In their rooms, they changed into dry clothes.

For supper Henry heated chili, Jessie set the table, Violet made a salad, and Benny arranged crackers on a plate.

James Alden came home just in time for dinner. "This looks delicious," he said, sitting down and rubbing his hands. He smiled at his grandchildren. "I like your snowman! But tell me, what else did you do today?"

Jessie told him about the mystery man, Violet described the newspaper article she found, Benny told about Carl and Alex's ring, and Henry explained the green ink that was used on both the article and the map.

Grandfather nodded wisely. "Well, there are a lot of suspects. With you and the police working on the case, you're sure to find the guilty person." He reached for a cracker. "Be careful, though. William Murray is concerned, too. We don't want you to be in any danger."

"I don't think we're in any danger, Grandfather," said Henry, spooning up the last of his chili.

"We want to find Mrs. Murray's diamonds," Jessie said. "But it's very confusing!"

"Maybe tomorrow night at the performance all the pieces will fall into place," Grandfather reassured them.

Benny shook his head. "I'm about ready to give up! Everyone could be a thief." He counted on his fingers. "First there's Marcia.

Then there's Janet and Ollie and the mystery man!"

"For all we know, it could even be Alex or Carl," Jessie said. "We can't eliminate them totally."

Henry smiled at Benny. "Since when do we give up, Benny? We'll find the thief! Now it's time for dessert." He brought in a chocolate cake. Jessie cut five slices.

Grandfather said, "I know you will! By the way, today I received a call from Joe and Alice."

Violet's eyes sparkled. "Where are they?"

"Did they find Soo Lee?" Jessie asked.

"When will they come home?" said Benny, through a mouthful of cake.

James Alden leaned back in his chair. "One question at a time. Soo Lee is with Joe and Alice in San Francisco. The Greenfield airport is still closed, but by Saturday the runway should be cleared and planes will be able to land."

"Saturday will be a glad day and a sad day," Jessie murmured.

"Sad?" Henry inquired, raising his brows. "Why?"

"Well," said Jessie, "we'll be glad to welcome Joe, Alice, and Soo Lee home, but sad because the ice skating troupe will be leaving for Cincinnati."

"That's true," Violet agreed. "But still, I can't wait to meet Soo Lee!"

Benny said thoughtfully, "I wonder if Soo Lee plays Monopoly."

Jessie smiled. "If she doesn't, we'll teach her. Grandfather, does Soo Lee speak English?"

Grandfather replied, "Alice said Soo Lee had learned English from a woman in the orphanage." Then he said, "Tomorrow is a big day. Aren't you baking cookies to sell at the benefit performance?"

"Yes, we have a lot to do," Henry said. "We're going to the Civic Center in the morning."

"I promised Carl I'd mend his shirt," Violet said, "and help Alex with her costume."

Henry piled several plates together. "Let's

clear the table, wash the dishes, and then bake cookies."

"Baking cookies is fun!" Benny said as he helped Jessie bring dishes into the kitchen. Violet and Henry washed and dried them.

Once the kitchen was clean, Henry opened the cookbook to two recipes — one for jam thumbprint cookies, and the other for gingerbread men.

"First," Violet said, "let's bake jam thumbprint cookies. They're pretty and will be perfect for the holidays!"

Jessie mixed the sugar and butter, then Violet added the eggs. Henry measured flour and stirred it in. After they'd let the dough chill, they all helped form it into little balls.

Once the cookie balls were on the metal sheet, ready for baking, Henry asked, "Now who wants to press down the center of the dough with your thumb?"

"Let me! Let me!" Benny said in a loud voice, holding up his thumb. "I've got a good thumb."

"All right, Benny," Jessie said, "go ahead."

Benny loved this part of the recipe best of all. Carefully, he pressed each cookie with his thumb.

Then Jessie filled each dent with a spoonful of raspberry jam.

While the thumbprint cookies baked, Violet mixed flour, ginger, molasses, sugar, and eggs for the gingerbread men. Henry rolled out the dough. Using the cookie cutter, Jessie cut out the gingerbread men.

While the cookies baked, the Aldens sat around the table and played Who Am I? Jessie thought of George Washington. Henry guessed Washington on the second clue.

When the stove timer buzzed, Jessie removed the baked cookies.

Violet filled the pastry tube with white frosting. She added a happy face to each gingerbread man.

After covering each tray with foil, Henry stretched. "I'm tired."

"Me, too," Jessie said, wiping a smudge of flour off her arm.

"Me, three." Benny gave a big yawn.

"Let's take our showers and go to bed," Violet suggested, heading for the stairs.

That night Benny snuggled deep under the covers. He smiled, thinking of his idea. He had a wonderful plan! *He* might be the one who would capture the thief all by himself.

CHAPTER 9

Green Ink

The next morning, as soon as Benny arrived at the Civic Center, he picked up a program for the night's performance. Next he went down to the edge of the rink.

"Carl!" Benny called to the skater who practiced a camel spin in the middle of the ice, "would you come here?"

Jessie had warned Benny not to upset Carl's practice, but Carl skated over to Benny. "What can I do for you?"

"Would you sign this?" Benny asked, holding out the program to Carl.

"Sure thing!" Carl said. "I'd feel honored. Do you have a pen?"

Benny shook his head. "No, sorry."

"I've got one right here," Carl said, skating to a bench where his jacket lay.

In fine handwriting he signed, "To Benny, a wonderful friend, Carl Underhill."

Benny hugged the program to his chest. "Thanks, Carl."

With a friendly wave at the Aldens, Carl skated away. No sooner was Carl gone, than Alex glided up to Benny. She gave him a teasing smile. "Aren't you going to ask for *my* autograph?"

"Yes! yes!" Benny said. "I wanted you next, Alex!" He pointed to her name on the program. "Will you sign here?"

"Be happy to," she said, skating to her gym bag on a bench and pulling out a pen.

Benny's eyes grew big and his smile turned upside down. "Th-that's a green pen," he stammered.

Alex smiled. "Is something wrong with a green pen?"

"No," Benny said, but his heart sank.

Alex signed her name, and Benny frowned. It was just what he was afraid of. The ink was green! "Thanks, Alex," he said in an unhappy voice.

"You're welcome!" Alex answered, skating to join Carl.

Benny took a deep breath, wishing Alex's pen hadn't been green. He went off to get Janet O'Shea's autograph, but she didn't have a pen and didn't have time to find one. Then he asked the mystery man but he wouldn't sign, either. He shook his head. Maybe his idea was dumb!

When Ollie came by, Benny asked him for his autograph, too. Ollie pulled a pen out of his hair and printed his name. Benny's eyes widened.

Each letter was in a different color:

O	L	L	I	E
yellow	red	orange	blue	green

"What a weird pen!" Benny exclaimed.

"It can write in different colors!"

"Here's one for you!" Ollie said with a big wink, pulling a second pen from his wig and tossing it to Benny. Then the clown slipped and slid his way across the rink.

"What are you up to, Benny?" asked Violet. "I think you're after *more* than skaters' signatures!"

"You'll see," Benny said. He didn't want to tell anyone his plans — not even Violet. Especially if it didn't work.

Jessie and Henry set up tables for their cookie sale, while Violet hurried backstage. "I almost forgot to mend Carl's shirt," she murmured.

Once in the dressing room, Violet settled into a back nook, hidden by hanging costumes.

She wasn't there long when someone entered. Violet peeked around the corner and drew in a sharp breath. Marcia propped her crutches against the wall, then hunched her shoulders and rotated her arms in a relaxing motion. "I'll be glad to throw these things

in the lake!" she muttered, glaring at her crutches.

Violet's eyes grew big. Without her crutches, Marcia walked across the big room to her green costume that hung on the wall. She closely examined the glittering material, making sure the buttons were on tight. Then she held the costume up to her.

Violet, careful not to make a sound, sat very still. Marica must not know she was here.

Finally, Marcia turned to leave. She tucked her crutches under her arms, and hobbled out to the rink.

Thoughtfully, Violet bit her lip. Didn't Marcia need crutches?

She hurried to tell Benny, Jessie, and Henry. "I just saw Marcia walk without crutches!" Violet said breathlessly.

Jessie looked across the rink, "But look at Marcia now! She's limping alongside Carl as innocently as you please. Maybe she's just getting better. But if she's the thief, I can understand why she pretends to need crutches. It's the perfect alibi!"

"I'm going to get Marcia's autograph!" Benny said, jumping up.

"Do you need to, Benny?" Henry said. "We should discuss Marcia and her crutches."

"I need to!" Benny said in a firm voice, dashing out.

Marcia turned her back when she saw Benny rushing toward her.

"Marcia!" Benny yelled. "Wait!"

She half-turned, impatiently tossing her red curls. "I don't have time to chat."

"This won't take long," Benny said, thrusting the program under her nose. "Please. Won't you sign this? I've got most of the other skaters' autographs."

"Oh," Marcia said with a sudden smile. "If that's all you want, I'd be glad to sign." She held out her hand. "Give me a pen?"

Benny patted his pocket. "Ooops, I forgot mine. Don't you have one?"

Marcia sighed. She hobbled over to her tote bag and fished out a pen.

Signing her name with a flourish, she said, "There! Marcia Westerly." She swung away on her crutches.

Benny stared at Marcia's green signature. He couldn't ask for better than this! "Wait until you see what I've got!" he crowed to his brother and sisters, waving the program high over his head.

Henry looked at Marcia's signature — written in green ink. "Benny! You're a real detective!"

Benny glowed at the praise.

"Now we know Marica doesn't need crutches and could easily climb in a window!" Jessie stated, "and she also owns a green ink pen." She smiled at Benny. "I'm proud of you!"

Benny stared at his feet. "But Alex and Ollie had green pens, too."

"Alex had a green pen?" Jessie asked. "And Ollie, too?"

Benny nodded.

"Benny," Violet said, "you had a good idea! All we need are more clues."

"Yes," Henry agreed, "we can't accuse Marcia or Alex or Ollie unless we can prove one of them stole Mrs. Murray's jewels." He hated to hear that Alex used green ink!

For a moment the children sat, deep in thought.

"Just because Alex and Ollie and Marcia wrote with green ink," Jessie said, "doesn't prove they're guilty."

Benny frowned. "No, but it could."

"And what about the mystery man?" Violet asked.

"And Janet O'Shea?" Henry added. "Did you get their signatures?"

Benny shook his head. "I guess you're right, but I still think it helps to see who had green ink."

"I have an idea, too!" Violet said, leaping up.

"Tell us," Jessie coaxed.

Henry gave Violet a questioning look, waiting patiently for her plan. When she didn't say anything, he said, "Well? What is it?"

Violet smiled mysteriously. "I'll tell you later."

"You don't want to tell us in case it doesn't work," Benny said.

"I'll be back in a minute," Violet said, hurrying toward Alex.

Jessie, Henry, and Benny watched as Violet whispered into Alex's ear.

Alex listened intently, then a quick smile lit her face, and she nodded in agreement.

"What are they talking about?" Benny asked, frowning. "I wish I could hear."

"We'll find out sooner or later," Henry said.

Whatever Violet had in mind, Jessie thought, Alex obviously thought it was a good idea. She watched them disappear inside the dressing room. She wished she were in on the secret.

CHAPTER 10

The Thief

Later that day at home, Jessie heated up some meatballs, while Henry boiled water, then dropped in spaghetti. Violet tossed a salad. Benny set the table, and got out some butter and Italian bread.

Grandfather had stayed in town to dine with the Murrays.

While the children ate, they discussed the newspaper article and map they'd found, plus the different suspects.

"I wonder if the police are any closer to finding the robber than we are," Violet said.

"I'll bet they don't know about the green ink!" Benny said proudly. "Marcia and Alex and Ollie are the only ones who wrote their names in green."

"Yes," Henry said, "that's an important clue, Benny, but we can't be sure any one of them is guilty." He buttered a slice of bread, then looked at Violet thoughtfully. "I know you have a plan. What is it?"

"I can't say," Violet said. "I just don't know how it will work out."

"When will we know?" Benny asked.

Violet laughed. "Before the performance, I promise."

"Speaking of performance," said Jessie, "we'd better clear the table and get dressed. We need to be at the Civic Center early so we can sell cookies."

"I can't wait to see the skaters!" said Benny. "They'll look like stars skating across the ice."

"They *are* stars," Henry said.

After leaving the kitchen spic and span, the excited Aldens went upstairs to dress.

Each could hardly wait to see the show.

Jessie brushed her brown hair until it shone. Violet came into Jessie's room to borrow a barrette.

"I see you're wearing your favorite dress," Jessie said, smiling.

Violet looked down at her lavender dress with a purple knit vest. "I want to look my best tonight," she said.

"Me, too," Jessie said, slipping an arm around Violet.

Downstairs, Henry winked at Violet. "We'd better leave, so Violet can try out her secret plan."

When they got to the Civic Center, they arranged cookies on trays. It wasn't long before people who arrived early had purchased a whole trayful of gingerbread men.

When Mr. and Mrs. Murray and James Alden came in, they went directly to the children. William Murray bought a dozen thumbprint cookies.

So did Grandfather. "For a snack later tonight," he said.

"You look so shiny," Benny said, gazing at Mrs. Murray.

"Why, thank you, Benny," Sara Murray said. Her white silk dress matched her white hair.

"Did you find your stolen diamonds?" Benny asked, staring at Mrs. Murray's sparking diamond earrings, necklace, bracelet, and rings.

Mrs. Murray laughed, touching one dangling earring. "No, no, my real diamonds and rubies are still missing. These are only paste."

"You mean you pasted on all that jewelry?" Benny questioned.

William Murray laughed. "Paste jewelry means fake jewelry. The diamonds that Sara is wearing tonight aren't real." Still smiling, he added, "I wish they were."

"Children, why don't you run along? Let us sell the rest of your cookies," Mrs. Murray said.

"Yes," Grandfather said. "The gingerbread men have all been sold and there are only a few of the thumbprint cookies left. Besides, I know you would like to see the ice skaters backstage before they begin their performance."

"Thanks," Jessie said. "I would like to see Alex."

The children left, knowing their cookie sale was in good hands.

"Mrs. Murray's diamonds look real. They didn't look like glue at all," Benny said.

"The word is paste, Benny." Henry chuckled. "Not glue!"

"Paste jewels," Benny repeated. "I forgot."

In the dressing room Alex was still in her practice outfit — leotards and T-shirt.

Jessie wondered why Alex wasn't dressed yet, but didn't ask. "I wanted to wish you good luck," she said.

Alex smiled, hugging Jessie. "Thanks, I think everything will be fine." She glanced at Violet. "Don't you think everything will work out, Violet?"

Violet replied, "I'm sure it will."

Carl poked his head in. He was dressed in red trousers and a sequined shirt. "Aren't you ready, Alex?"

"In a few minutes," she answered.

"We're on in fifteen minutes," Carl said, leaving.

Suddenly, Alex exclaimed. "Oh, Violet. Look at my costume! It's ripped!"

"You can't possibly wear it like that," Violet said, examining the short red dress.

Alex looked at Marcia, who sat in a corner reading a magazine. "Since you're not skating, Marcia," Alex said, "could I please wear your green dress?"

Marcia jumped up, forgetting her crutches. "No!" Then she added in a calmer voice, "It wouldn't fit you. You're smaller than I am." She reached for the costume, but Violet quickly took it off the hanger.

"I can fix that," Violet said. "A stitch here and there and it will be perfect."

Marcia bit her lip, not knowing what to say. Finally she said in a weak tone, "Be careful of it!"

"Of course," Alex answered, going behind a folding screen with Violet.

Marcia glared at Jessie, Henry, and Benny. "If anything happens to that dress," she muttered, "I'll . . . I'll . . ."

Henry gave her a puzzled frown. "Why are you so nervous about a costume?"

"Yes, why are you, Marcia?" Alex asked, re-emerging from the screen with Violet. "I don't think I'll be wearing your dress, after all."

Violet held up the green dress. In the light the rhinestones and other stones glittered and sparkled.

"Those diamonds and rubies don't look like *paste*," Benny said. "They look real!"

"I think they are," Violet said in a quiet voice. "Aren't they, Marcia?"

Marcia stood rooted to the spot, not speaking. Her hands trembled as she reached for her crutches.

"I don't think you need these anymore," Henry said, moving Marcia's crutches away from her.

"Well, Marcia?" Alex said.

Just then Carl came in. "Are you ready, Alex? There's not much time . . ." He stared at the bright stones on the green dress, then at Marcia without her crutches.

"I think we've caught our thief," Violet said.

CHAPTER 11

Confession

Marcia stood defiantly facing Violet and Alex. "Are you accusing me of the jewel robbery?" she asked. "You have no proof."

"This is proof!" Violet said, holding up Marcia's green costume.

Marcia stared at her costume. She said nothing.

"I'll be right back," Jessie whispered to Henry. In a few minutes she returned with Grandfather, Janet O'Shea, the Murrays —

and the mystery man. They all crowded into the dressing room.

"The police have been called," Jessie said. She glanced at Marcia, feeling sorry for her, yet angry, too. How could she have stolen Mrs. Murray's jewels?

Marcia glared at Violet.

Puzzled, Mrs. Murray looked around. "Are my jewels here? I don't see them."

Without a word, Violet handed Mrs. Murray the green costume.

Mrs. Murray looked from the green dress to Violet, then back at the dress. Suddenly she gasped. "My diamonds and rubies! I'd recognize their sparkle and cut anywhere! William, look!"

Mr. Murray studied the gems. "These *are* our jewels," he announced. "Each one has been removed from its setting and put into a clasp that holds buttons, then sewn onto the costume."

Benny's mouth formed a big O. "You mean the jewels were in plain sight all the time — the buttons are the jewels!"

"That's right," Alex said. "Violet thought it was strange that Marcia was so careful of her costume, checking the stones to be certain they were secure."

"When I saw Marcia without her crutches," Violet said, "and then saw her study her costume, I became suspicious." She glanced at Marcia. "You see, I was sewing in a corner in the back when you came into the dressing room today and leaned your crutches against the wall."

Marcia's expression was grim. "So you saw me walk and look at my costume." She shrugged. "That doesn't mean I'm a thief!"

"Don't forget you used green ink!" Benny shouted. "That was another clue!"

"Yes," Alex said, smiling. "But I wrote in green ink, too! And so did Ollie."

"I knew you couldn't steal anything!" Benny answered.

"Green ink?" Marcia repeated. "What are you talking about?"

Henry pulled papers from his pocket. "You used green ink on this map and also on the newspaper article." He put a hand on Benny's shoulder. "When Benny got your autograph, he realized that you and Alex and Ollie had pens with green ink."

Sighing, Marcia dropped into a chair.

"We decided to play a trick on you," Alex said.

Marcia stared at Alex. "Do you mean your costume wasn't torn?"

"Not even a little," Alex replied. "But we needed to look at yours. We suspected you'd sewn on the real jewels."

The man in black stepped forward, smoothing his mustache. He cleared his throat and spoke in a deep voice: "Marcia Westerly, you've not only stolen Mrs. Murray's jewels, but also robbed homes in Albany, Philadelphia, and Pittsburg!"

"Who are you?" Benny asked, surprised the man knew so much.

Janet O'Shea spoke up. "This is Adam Hooper, a detective I hired."

Suddenly two policemen squeezed into the room.

"This is the thief!" Adam Hooper announced, pointing at Marcia. "We're waiting for her explanation."

"I'm Officer Mylansky," the bigger of the two men said, "and this is my partner, Officer Greene." He flipped open a notepad. "Who found the jewels?"

Adam Hooper sheepishly turned to the Aldens. "I can't take credit. The Aldens pieced together the whole thing."

Marcia's mouth became a thin line, and she said in a cold tone, "Yes, the clever Aldens! If it hadn't been for them, I'd have been on a plane tomorrow, and no one would have been the wiser. I've always wanted to have money. I was going to sell the jewels when I got out of this town." She added bitterly, "The blizzard was against me, too! Snow closed the airport, or I would have left town the day after the robbery!"

"Did you really burglarize homes in those other cities?" Henry asked, disbelief on his face.

"Yes, I did!' Marcia stood up, facing her

accusers. "It was easy. My crutches gave me the perfect excuse." She paused, glancing at the waiting officers. "The Murrays' house was going to be my last robbery with the troupe. I knew I couldn't stay on crutches forever!"

"No, you couldn't!" Janet exclaimed. I was beginning to wonder when you were *ever* going to put on a pair of skates! To think I hired you!"

"I wondered about you, too, Marcia," Jessie said, "when you didn't know a simple skating term or who Valentina Markov was!"

Marcia gave a bitter laugh. "I guess I gave myself away in more ways than one!"

"Come along, Miss," Officer Greene said, leading Marcia out of the room.

Mrs. Murray clutched the green dress, examining each gem. "Every diamond and ruby has been fastened on this dress." Tears filled her eyes. "How can I thank everyone!"

For a moment all that was heard was the police siren fading into the distance, then

Benny spoke up, "You could buy the rest of our cookies!"

Mr. Murray put his arm around his wife. "We will, we will!" he promised, laughing.

"And we'll put on the best ice show you've ever seen!" said Carl. He touched Alex's hand, and she smiled at him. "I'll be ready in five minutes," she said.

All at once, Janet O'Shea waved a paper overhead. "I have more good news! The tickets to our five Cincinnati performances are completely sold out!" She smiled. "It looks as if all my skaters will be paid, and get bonuses, too!"

Benny tilted his head. "It's the first time I ever saw you smile, Miss O'Shea."

Janet O'Shea chuckled. "I haven't had much to smile about! I think, though, sunny skies are ahead!"

"Good!" Benny said. "Then you can smile all the time."

Everyone laughed, and, except for the skaters, they hurried to take their seats for the performance.

Bugles blared. The arena darkened, then one spotlight shone. Ollie Olsen came careening out on the ice on his stomach, sliding across the rink.

Benny laughed the hardest at Ollie's funny routine. The clown stumbled around the rink, stopping in front of Benny and doffing his hat. He shook his head from side to side, which caused his orange wig to slip over one eye. He pulled a fuzzy rabbit from his sleeve, then presented it to Benny.

Benny's eyes shone. "Thank you!" he said, hugging the rabbit.

Ollie, plopping his hat back on, teetered back and forth. With a bow so low his round false nose touched the ice, he whirled about, tripping and tottering offstage.

Soft music played and the spotlight moved to a couple skimming around the rink. Alex and Carl, in red, glittering costumes, skated out to the middle. They did double and triple jumps, and when Carl lifted Alex high overhead, Jessie clapped the loudest. "Aren't they wonderful?" she said to Henry.

"The best," he replied.

More skaters came out. With the colored lights, music, and costumes, the show was one of the most beautiful sights the Aldens had ever seen. The performers' intricate footwork and spins were breathtaking.

"I want to be an ice skater when I grow up!" Benny exclaimed.

Violet smiled. "Maybe you will, Benny. Maybe you will."

Jessie and Henry smiled, too, knowing Benny would change his mind many times before he grew up.

On the way home, the children sat quietly in the car, enjoying the way the moonlight sparkled on the white snow.

In his pajamas, Henry touched his toes twenty-five times. It had been a busy day. A thief had been caught, the jewels had been returned to Mrs. Murray, and they'd seen an ice show more spectacular than any they'd ever imagined. Tomorrow, they'd meet Soo Lee. He switched off the light and climbed into bed. What could be better?

CHAPTER 12

Soo Lee

As the Aldens ate their breakfast, they admired the gifts they'd chosen for Soo Lee. Henry had bought a lovely illustrated Cinderella book; Violet, a doll dressed in a denim skirt and plaid blouse; Jessie, a soft teddy bear; and Benny, a bright red fire engine.

"Could I have another piece of toast?" Benny asked. "It's a long way to the airport."

"Sure," Henry said, popping a slice in the toaster.

Grandfather pushed back his chair. "I'm

proud of each of you for solving the Murrays' robbery. Sara is very happy. Your ideas worked!"

"The green-ink idea was mine," Benny said, heaping a tablespoon of jam on his toast.

"I won't forget," Grandfather said with a chuckle. He glanced at his watch. "We'd better leave for the airport. The Starlight Troupe will be leaving soon, and I know you want to say good-bye."

Jessie jumped up. "I don't want to miss Alex!"

Benny said, "I don't want to see the ice skaters leave."

"None of us do," Jessie said softly.

"I'm sure they'll come back," Henry said in a reassuring tone.

Benny brightened again. "Really?"

"Really," Jessie said. "And if they don't, I'll bet Grandfather will take us to a city where they're performing!"

"Yes, Grandfather would do that, wouldn't he," Benny said, putting on his jacket. He felt better.

When they arrived at the airport, Alex and Carl rushed to meet them. "We were afraid you wouldn't get here on time," Carl said. He raised Benny high in the air.

Benny shouted with delight.

Alex turned to Jessie. "Will you write to me? I want to hear how your skating lessons are going."

"Of course," Jessie said, trying to swallow away the lump in her throat.

Alex hugged Jessie and Violet. She looked at Henry, reaching for his hands, and hugged him, too.

Henry's ears reddened, but he smiled with pleasure.

Alex turned to Benny, but before she could hug him, he stuck out his hand. "Good-bye, Alex," he said. "I don't like mushy stuff."

Alex smiled, gravely shaking his hand.

Janet O'Shea motioned to her skaters. "Hurry! They've called our flight. Ollie and the others are already on the plane." With a wave, she hurried away.

Carl's voice was firm. "We'll never forget the Aldens!" He spun about, grabbing Alex's hand. They disappeared down the ramp to the plane.

With sadness, Jessie watched the Starlight Troupe's plane taxi down the runway, then lift into the air. But as soon as their plane was out of sight, another plane circled the airfield, then landed.

"Joe and Alice are on that plane!" Henry exclaimed.

"And Soo Lee!" Benny shouted.

At the gate, the Aldens watched eagerly as the passengers emerged. All at once, Joe and Alice came down the passageway holding the hands of a small Korean girl.

"Over here!" shouted Henry.

Joe and Alice hurried toward them.

They hugged each of the Aldens, then, smiling, said, "This is our daughter."

Soo Lee's big dark eyes were solemn as she gazed at the Aldens.

"Hi, Soo Lee," Jessie said, bending over. "Did you have a good trip?"

"Yes, thank you," Soo Lee said. She gave Jessie a shy smile.

"Let's get your bags," James Alden said. "I have the station wagon, and we'll stop at our house for hot chocolate."

"We'd have been here two days ago," Alice said, "except for the blizzard."

"Yes, but the blizzard helped us catch a thief," Benny piped up.

Joe gave Benny a sharp look. "A thief?"

"We'll tell you the whole story," Henry said, "in the car."

When James Alden pulled into the driveway, everyone piled out.

Joe said, "What an adventure you had, Benny!"

"It was exciting!" Benny exclaimed, "but I'm glad we found out who robbed the Murrays, and I'm really glad you're home!"

"So are we!" Alice said emphatically. "It was a long trip."

Over hot chocolate and cookies, Joe told of their wait in Seoul, Korea, for Soo Lee.

"You should have seen the papers we

signed," Alice said, shaking her head. She reached over and put her hand over Soo Lee's. "But it was worth it."

Benny, sitting next to Soo Lee, turned to her and said, "Do you play Monopoly?"

"No, but thank you."

"I don't think Soo Lee knows what Monopoly is," Joe said.

"Is it food?" Soo Lee asked.

"Monopoly is a game," Benny said with an encouraging smile. "I'll teach you."

Soo Lee smiled and her dark eyes shone. "Good. I would like that."

"She learns fast," Joe warned. "She'll beat you soon."

Jessie presented Soo Lee with a package. Opening the box, Soo Lee smiled. She held the teddy bear tightly in her arms.

Henry and Violet gave her their gifts. "For me?" Soo Lee pointed at herself.

"Yes," Grandfather said. "The children wanted to make your homecoming special."

Soo Lee admired the doll and the book. When she opened the fire truck Benny had

given her, her smile broadened. "I like this," she said, getting off the chair and rolling the truck back and forth on the carpet.

"I'm glad you like it," Benny said. He laughed when Soo Lee pushed a button and the fire truck's siren went off. "We're going to have lots of fun together," he said.

Jessie, Henry, and Violet thought so, too.

GERTRUDE CHANDLER WARNER discovered when she was teaching that many readers who like an exciting story could find no books that were both easy and fun to read. She decided to try to meet this need, and her first book, *The Boxcar Children*, quickly proved she had succeeded.

Miss Warner drew on her own experiences to write each mystery. As a child she spent hours watching trains go by on the tracks opposite her family home. She often dreamed about what it would be like to set up housekeeping in a caboose or freight car — the situation the Alden children find themselves in.

When Miss Warner received requests for more adventures involving Henry, Jessie, Violet, and Benny Alden, she began additional stories. In each, she chose a special setting and introduced unusual or eccentric characters who liked the unpredictable.

While the mystery element is central to each of Miss Warner's books, she never thought of them as strictly juvenile mysteries. She liked to stress the Aldens' independence and resourcefulness and their solid New England devotion to using up and making do. The Aldens go about most of their adventures with as little adult supervision as possible — something else that delights young readers.

Miss Warner lived in Putnam, Connecticut, until her death in 1979. During her lifetime, she received hundreds of letters from girls and boys telling her how much they liked her books.